For Tom and Catherine — our treasure
E. G.

To Mama and Papa
J. T.

First U.S. edition 2018

Library of Congress Catalog Card Number pending
ISBN 978-0-7636-9644-3

17 18 19 20 21 22 WKT 10 9 8 7 6 5 4 3 2 1

Printed in Shenzhen, Guangdong, China

This book was typeset in Tw Cen MT.
The illustrations were created digitally.

Nosy Crow
an imprint of
Candlewick Press
99 Dover Street
Somerville, Massachusetts 02144

www.nosycrow.com
www.candlewick.com

The Treasure of Pirate Frank

Mal Peet and
Elspeth Graham

illustrated by
Jez Tuya

nosy crow

An imprint of Candlewick Press

This is the boy who wants to find
the treasure of Pirate Frank.

This is the **map**
that shows the way
to the **treasure**
of Pirate Frank.

ISLAND OF S

SEA

SNOWY
MOUNTAINS

FOREST

N
W   E
S

This is the **sea** that must be sailed.

It's on the **map** that shows the way
to the **treasure of Pirate Frank.**

There's the **island** of spice and gold
beyond the **sea** that must be sailed.

It's on the **map** that shows the way
to the **treasure of Pirate Frank.**

These are the **mountains** snowy and cold
on the **island** of spice and gold
beyond the **sea** that must be sailed.

They're on the **map** that shows the way
to the **treasure of Pirate Frank.**

Here's the forest where monkeys swing
over the **mountains** snowy and cold
on the **island** of spice and gold
beyond the **sea** that must be sailed.

It's on the map that shows the way
to the treasure of Pirate Frank.

This is the swamp where bullfrogs sing
past the forest where monkeys swing
over the mountains snowy and cold
on the island of spice and gold
beyond the sea that must be sailed.

It's on the **map**
that shows the way
to the **treasure**
of Pirate Frank.

Here are the **steps** going higher and higher
above the **swamp** where bullfrogs sing
past the **forest** where monkeys swing
over the **mountains** snowy and cold
on the **island** of spice and gold
beyond the **sea** that must be sailed.

They're on the **map** that shows the way
to the **treasure of Pirate Frank.**

Here's the **volcano** that spits out fire
at the top of the **steps** going higher and higher
above the **swamp** where bullfrogs sing
past the **forest** where monkeys swing
over the **mountains** snowy and cold
on the **island** of spice and gold
beyond the **sea** that must be sailed.

It's on the **map** that shows the way
to the **treasure of** Pirate Frank.

There's the tall tree that marks the spot
beside the volcano that spits out fire
at the top of the steps going higher and higher
above the swamp where bullfrogs sing
past the forest where monkeys swing
over the mountains snowy and cold
on the island of spice and gold
beyond the sea that must be sailed.

It's on the **map** that shows the way
to the **treasure of Pirate Frank.**

And under the **tree** that marks the spot is . . .

Pirate Frank!

She's not on the map!

Quick! Run!
Down the steps
going lower, not higher,
below the volcano
that spits out fire . . .

through the swamp
where bullfrogs sing . . .

through the **forest**

where monkeys swing . . .

over the **mountains**

snowy and cold . . .

and off the **island**
of spice and gold,
into the ship, to sail away . . .

and dream of what was found today . . .

the treasure of Pirate Frank.